First published 2015 by A & C Black,
an imprint of Bloomsbury Publishing Plc
50 Bedford Square, London, WC1B 3DP

www.bloomsbury.com

Bloomsbury is a registered trademark of Bloomsbury Publishing Plc

A CIP catalogue for this book is available from the British Library

ISBN 978-1-4729-1196-4

Typeset by Newgen Knowledge Works (P) Ltd., Chennai, India

Printed and bound in Great Britain by CPI Group (UK) Ltd,
Croydon, CR0 4YY

1 3 5 7 9 10 8 6 4 2

recommended by
CatchUp®
www.catchup.org

Catch Up is a charity which
aims to address the problem of
underachievement that has its roots
in literacy and numeracy difficulties.

ANDY CROFT

ILLUSTRATED BY
Sean Longcroft

A & C BLACK
AN IMPRINT OF BLOOMSBURY
LONDON NEW DELHI NEW YORK SYDNEY

To the pupils and staff of
Grewelthorpe Primary School

Contents

Chapter One

Mad Max

"Ladies and gentlemen, boys and girls,
welcome to the circus!
Enjoy the music!
Laugh at the clowns!
Watch the acrobats fly!
Be amazed by the animals!"

Max held out a big plastic hula-hoop and set fire to it with a match. The orange and black tabby cat sitting on the garden chair didn't move.

"Come on, Fluffy," whispered Max. "Jump through the hula-hoop! You're supposed to be a lion."

The cat yawned and closed her eyes.

"Jump, you stupid cat!" shouted Max. The flames were getting close to Max's hand. He could feel the heat.

"Jump before I... ow!" Max dropped the burning hula-hoop on the grass. "Ow, ow, ow!" he yelled, hopping about and holding his burnt hand.

"Max, have you seen my hula-hoop?" called his little sister, Lily.

"Your hula-hoop? Er... no," said Max. He hoped Lily wouldn't see the burnt hula-hoop on the lawn.

"Max, why are you holding your hand like that? Have you hurt yourself?" asked Lily.

"Not really," pretended Max. "I was just playing with Fluffy. I think she scratched me."

"Bad Fluffy, hurting Max," said Lily as she picked up the cat and cuddled it.

"Put Fluffy down," said Max.
"We're busy."

Lily put the cat down. Fluffy looked at
Max, then jumped over the wall into the
next-door neighbour's garden.

Just then, their mum came into the
garden to hang up some clothes on the
washing-line.

"Mum, have you seen my hula-hoop?" asked Lily.

"Well, I saw Max with it a few minutes ago," she replied.

Mum put down the washing-basket and sniffed the garden air.

"Has something been burning?" she asked. "What have you been doing, Max? What's happened to your hand?"

"And what's that funny mark on the grass?" asked Lily, pointing to the burnt black ring next to Max. "What's happened to my hula-hoop?"

Lily started crying.

"Look Mum, I can explain…" Max began.

"I don't want to hear it, Max," said his mum. "You can go to your bedroom. Now! And you can buy Lily a new hula-hoop."

"That's not fair!" said Max.

But Mum just pointed to the house with a cross look on her face.

Max went to his bedroom and sat on his bed.

"If I were a real lion-tamer, I would have a real lion and not a stupid old cat," he thought.

"And I would practise in a circus, not in a back-garden."

Chapter Two

Chicken and Egg

When Max was eight years old, his parents had taken him to the circus. He thought it was the best thing ever. There was a tightrope walker and a juggler. There were acrobats, clowns and trapeze artists. There was a sword-swallower, a fire-eater and a knife-thrower. Max loved it!

Ever since that day, Max had been
practising his circus act. He needed to
be ready.

He couldn't just turn up at a circus one
day and expect them to give him a job.

The only problem was that Max was
very clumsy. He was always breaking things,
hurting himself and getting into trouble.

Even his best friends thought Max was a
bit of a wally.

At first, Max wanted to be a magician.
He borrowed a book of magic-tricks from
the library. He practised some of the tricks
for ages. He tried to make a pound-coin
disappear between his fingers. But he kept
dropping the coin.

He tried to make a playing card appear
in his hand. But the card always seemed to
stick in his sleeve.

Max's magic tricks got him into a lot
of trouble.

He wanted to wear a top hat like the
magician in the circus, so he borrowed a hat
his mum had once worn at a wedding.

He put Fluffy into the hat. Fluffy quite liked it in the hat and she settled down for a sleep. But Mum went mad when she found that her best hat was full of cat hairs.

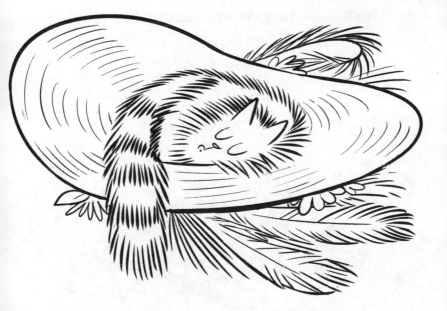

Max gave up trying to become a
magician. He decided to be a juggler instead.

He found some old tennis-balls in the
garden-shed and started practising. But
Mum went mad when he broke the kitchen
window. So he gave up juggling.

Max tried spinning a set of plates on some sticks but they all fell to the ground and smashed into pieces.

It turned out they were his mum's best plates.

Max decided to be a circus acrobat. He tried to do a handstand on Lily's rocking horse. But he fell off and hurt his wrist. He also broke the rocking horse's head.

Lily went crying to Mum. She went mad again. Now Max had to save his pocket money to get the rocking horse fixed.

Max gave up the idea of being an acrobat.

Next, Max thought he would try being a hypnotist. "I'm going to turn you into a chicken," he said to Lily.

"I don't want to be a chicken," said Lily. "Why can't you turn me into a cat?"

"Be quiet," said Max.

Max stared at Lily. "Look into my eyes," he said. "When I count to ten, you will be a chicken." And Max began counting: "One, two, three…"

"But what if Fluffy tries to eat me?" asked Lily.

"Don't be silly. Fluffy is not going to eat you. Four, five, six…" went on Max.

"Why don't you turn Fluffy into a chicken?" said Lily.

"Seven, eight, nine…" counted Max.

"If you turn Fluffy into a chicken then we could all have fresh eggs for breakfast!" said Lily.

"Ten!" Max finished counting.

But Lily had gone to find Fluffy.

"I wish I could really make Lily disappear," thought Max crossly.

One day, Max took down a large suitcase from the top of the wardrobe in his bedroom.

"What are you going to do with that?" asked Lily. "Turn it into a chicken?"

"I'm going to turn you into an escape-artist. Now stop talking and get inside."

"I'm not getting into that suitcase!" said Lily.

"Look Lily, I promise not to lock it."

"*You* get inside it, Max"

"I'm too big."

"Well what about Fluffy? She's even smaller than I am."

"But Fluffy isn't an escape-artist. She's a cat."

"Well, I'm not an escape artist, am I? I'm a girl. And I'm not going in that suitcase. So there." Lily opened the bedroom door.

"What are you doing?" asked Max.

"I'm escaping!" she said. And off she went.

Chapter Three

To the Max

Max asked his best friends, Paul and Mark, to come round after school. He wanted them to help him practise his circus act.

"What do we have to do?" asked Paul.

"Is it safe?" asked Mark.

"Of course it's safe," said Max. "All you have to do is catch me."

Max swung on the garden swing, as high as the swing would go. He was like an acrobat on a flying trapeze.

"Are you ready to catch me?" he shouted to Paul and Mark.

"Are you really sure this is safe?" shouted Mark again.

"Are you ready?" shouted Max.

"But what if...?" began Paul.

It was too late. Max let go of the swing and flew into the air. He flew across the garden and landed on top of Paul and Mark. They rolled over in a muddy heap of twisted arms and legs into the flowerbed.

For a few minutes no one spoke. They all lay there, trying to catch their breath.

"My head hurts," said Paul. "And my arm."

"So does my back," said Mark. "And my leg."

"I've got it!" yelled Max, sitting up. "I've got it!"

"What have you got?" asked Paul and Mark.

"A new idea!" said Max.

Paul and Mark looked at Max.

"I don't like the sound of this," said Mark.

"What is it?" asked Paul.

"Tight-rope walking," said Max excitedly.

"What?!" said Mark.

"You know,' said Max. "Walking across a rope, high above the ground, without falling off."

"No way!" said Mark and Paul together.

But Max was pointing to the
washing-line hung between two apple trees.

"I'm not walking on that," said Paul.

"You don't have to," said Max "All you
have to do is catch me if I fall off."

"No way!" said Mark and Paul again.

Max started climbing one of the apple trees.

"It can't be *that* hard," he said. "Just stand underneath me in case I slip. You don't want me to hurt myself, do you?"

Mark and Paul stood underneath the washing-line.

"Are you ready?" called Max.

The boys looked up. Max had one foot on the washing-line. He was still holding on to the trunk of the apple tree.

Just as Max was about to put his other foot on the washing-line, Fluffy came running out into the garden.

She ran up the apple tree. Max let go of the trunk, fell out of the tree and on to the washing-line.

The washing-line snapped. Max fell with a thud on top of Mark and Paul. They all rolled over into the flowerbed again.

"My arm hurts," said Paul. "And my head."

"So does my leg," said Mark. "And my arm."

Lily came into the garden and saw the boys in a heap in the flowerbed.

"What are you doing?" she asked.

"Are you playing hide and seek? Is Max going to lock you in a suitcase? Or turn you into a chicken?"

Mark and Paul didn't answer.

"I know!" said Max. "Let's try sword-swallowing!"

But Mark and Paul were already limping away down the garden path.

"Come back!" yelled Max after them. "Where are you going? We haven't tried knife-throwing yet. Or fire-eating..."

Chapter Four

Relax Max

Lily was lying in a big cardboard box in the kitchen. "But I don't like want to be cut in half!" she cried.

"It's not real," said Max. "It's a trick. You don't think I'm *really* going to saw you in half, do you?"

But Lily *did* think Max was going to saw her in half. And she didn't like the sound of that at all.

"Just relax," said Max. "Everything will be alright. You'll see."

Max pretended he was talking to an audience.

"Ladies and gentlemen, boys and girls," he said. "Get ready to be amazed. What you are about to see is a woman sawn in half."

"But I'm not a woman, I'm a little girl!" cried Lily. "And I don't want to be sawn in half!"

"Just stop talking and smile at the audience," insisted Max.

"But there's nobody here," said Lily.

Max ignored her. He picked up a rusty old saw and started cutting through the cardboard box.

"If you cut me in half," asked Lily "will there be two of me?"

"Of course not," said Max. "Now please stop talking. Sawing people is hard work, you know."

Max began sawing again. But the saw wasn't strong enough to cut through the thick cardboard box.

"I bet Fluffy could do a better job," said Lily.

"No, she couldn't!" snapped Max.

Max needed a bigger saw.

He ran to the garage and grabbed his Dad's electric power saw. He ran back to the kitchen but the kitchen was empty.

Lily had vanished… as if by magic!

Chapter Five

The Cat in the Hat

It was the day of the school talent show. Max had been practising his act for weeks. This was his chance to show everyone what he could do.

His mum and dad had tried to talk him out of entering the show. So had Paul and Mark. And Lily.

The school hall was packed with kids, teachers and parents. Max sat and waited for his turn. He was wearing his cousin's trousers. They were too big for him so he had borrowed a pair of his granddad's braces to hold them up. He had bought a cheap top hat and a fake beard from a joke shop.

The talent show started. A girl played the violin, Paul played the piano and some girls did a dance-routine. After each act, the audience clapped politely. Mark told some bad jokes and everyone groaned. The biggest cheer was for a rap performed by some of the older boys. It looked like they were going to win.

Finally, it was Max's turn. He stepped onto the stage. Everyone was watching him.

"Ladies and gentlemen, boys and girls..." he began. "Today, I bring you... the magic of the circus!"

The audience clapped. Max bowed.
As he did so, his beard fell off. One of the
teachers burst out laughing.

Max tried to stick the beard back on.
Then, he put the top hat on the table in front
of him and picked up his magic-wand. The
room went very quiet.

He was just about to say the magic words when the top hat began to move. Some kids began giggling. Max put the hat back in the middle of the table. But it moved again.

Suddenly, the hat jumped off the table and ran across the floor. The audience laughed and laughed.

Max ran after the hat. Everyone was really laughing now. They could see an orange and black tail sticking out from under the hat.

"Fluffy!" shouted Lily, as the cat wriggled out from under the top hat.

"Come back you stupid cat!" hissed Max as he chased after her.

But Fluffy didn't want to go back inside the hat. She began climbing the curtain at the side of the stage. Max stretched out to grab her. As he did so, his braces snapped and his trousers fell down.

The audience gave a cheer.

Max tried to pull his trousers up with one hand but he lost his balance. He grabbed the curtain to stop himself falling over, but the curtain fell down on top of him.

The audience were now roaring with laughter.

Max crawled out from under the curtain. Fluffy was sitting on his head. He stood up. His trousers were still round his ankles. He listened to the applause and the laughter.

"Yes!" he thought. "I've done it! The audience really love me."

This was the magic of the circus.

As Max took one final bow, his beard fell off again. Max knew at last what he was going to do when he was older. He was going to be a clown.